THE ADVENTURES
OF
ROBINSON CRUSOE

THE ADVENTURES OF ROBINSON CRUSOE

Daniel Defoe

Om Books International

First published in 2012 by

OM

Om Books International

Corporate & Editorial Office
A-12, Sector 64, Noida 201 301
Uttar Pradesh, India
Phone: +91 120 477 4100
Email: editorial@ombooks.com
Website: www.ombooksinternational.com

Sales Office
4379/4B, Prakash House, Ansari Road
Darya Ganj, New Delhi 110 002, India
Phone: +91 11 2326 3363, 2326 5303
Fax: +91 11 2327 8091
Email: sales@ombooks.com
Website: www.ombooks.com

Adapted by Subhojit Sanyal
Illustrations: Dipankar, Manoj Kumar Prasad
Design and Layout: Shraboni Roy

ISBN: 978-93-81607-74-9

Printed in India

10 9 8 7 6 5 4 3 2 1

Contents

Chapter One

Going Out to Sea

By the time he turned eighteen years old, young Robinson Crusoe had no intentions of studying law as per his father's wishes, and neither did he want to become a part of the family business, as his mother wanted him to be. All he wanted was to travel through the wide seas and live his life.

"Listen to me, my son," begged his father. "There is nothing to be gained by living at sea. You will only meet great disappointment and suffering."

But his father's stern tone, or even his pleading tears had no effect on Robinson Crusoe. "Please father! It has always been my dream to travel through the world. Please let me go on this one voyage and I promise that if I don't like it, I will surely come back to you and live in Yorkshire."

However, his parents would just not agree. Robinson was their son, and they were well aware of the dangers that the sea offered her travellers. There were storms that threw ships completely off their course, some storms even dragged them to the shore and split them into broken pieces of wood! And then of course, there were the pirates who frequently loot the cargo of merchant ships and deliver their crew to the hands of death. They were adamant that their son would, therefore, not seek a life at sea.

And thus Robinson continued living his life at Yorkshire, thinking of the sea and her mysteries in his dreams. A year later, he went to visit one of his friends at the seaport of Hull. The boy's father, the captain of a ship, invited Robinson Crusoe to join him on a short journey to London in his ship.

Naturally, it was an offer that Robinson could just not refuse.

Therefore, on the first of September, 1651, Robinson Crusoe started off on his maiden sea voyage, one that would take him to the distant shores of Africa, to South America and even a visit to an island in the Caribbean Sea, before he could return to England once more.

This was a great learning experience for young Robinson Crusoe. He lived through storms that made him seasick and he also realised how fierce and dangerous a storm at sea could actually be. He understood that when at sea, the ship and her men were always at the mercy of the dark storm clouds and their ravishing wind.

However, these fears died down the moment he came back to England and was on dry land once more. Therefore, he was soon on his way to the coast of Africa on his next voyage. This time too he learnt many new things about life at sea. He learnt what it felt like to be dealing with the natives of Africa, and when the ship was attacked and captured by pirates on their way back, he knew what real fear felt like. Robinson Crusoe had to serve as the pirate captain's slave, but luckily, he was able to escape in the captain's small fishing boat later with a few of his crewmen.

They were rescued by a Portuguese merchant ship, which was then on its way to Brazil in South America. Robinson Crusoe accompanied them to Brazil and during his stay there, he made his living by working at a sugar plantation. Few years later, Crusoe was able to save quite some money, with which he even managed to buy a sugar plantation of his own. His successful trade in the sugar plantation lasted for quite some years after that, and he made many friends during his stay in Brazil.

As the sugar plantation business expanded, the plantation owners realised that they would need a lot many new slaves, who would do all the hard work on the plantations. Since Robinson

Crusoe had earlier dealt with the natives in Africa, he was requested to travel to Africa and bring back slaves from there.

Giving up such a promising and large plantation business and sailing across the violent Atlantic Ocean was no small deed, but Robinson Crusoe geared up for the adventure, giving the responsibility of the plantation to his friends.

When he finally boarded the ship at Sao Salvador in Brazil on the first of September, 1659, Robinson Crusoe realised that it had been eight whole years since he had started off on his first sea voyage from Hull in England. Little did he know at the point of time, that he was setting sail for the greatest adventure of his... or anyone's life!

Chapter Two

Disaster at Sea

When the ship finally left Sao Salvador that morning, there were a total of fourteen people on board — the captain, twelve sea men, and of course, Robinson Crusoe. There was a huge cargo of toys on board too, ones that Crusoe intended to use as trade with the natives. There were various kinds of beads, shells, knives, hatchets and even little mirrors in the cargo hold.

The course of the ship was simple. They were to first head north, right till the northern tip of Brazil, from where the Captain would steer the ship across the Atlantic Ocean, into Africa.

By the twelfth day of their voyage, just as they were nearing the northern end of Brazil, a violent hurricane broke along the seas. It was vicious and just refused to calm down. For ten days, the ship sailed through the hurricane, in every possible direction that she was thrown. Two sailors were thrown overboard and one died because of tropical fever that the hurricane brought with it. Robinson Crusoe feared for the worst. As the sails and the masts ripped away, he was certain that the sea would soon turn into their graves.

It was only on the eleventh day that they finally sailed into calm seas again. The first thing that both Robinson Crusoe and the Captain did was check the ship for the damages caused by the hurricane. Of one thing they were both certain — that the ship would not be able to carry on with her voyage all the way to Africa. However, the Captain wanted to sail all the way back to Brazil, while Robinson Crusoe felt they should sail for one of the British islands in the Caribbean belt.

The island of Barbados was only a fifteen day sail and Crusoe felt it would be wiser to fix the ship there.

However, the seas turned violent once again, as a second hurricane poured through the skies. They were once again thrown off course, and were moving eastwards to islands known to be inhabited by savages, those who were yet to see the light of modern civilization.

The whole night was spent like it were a nightmare, with strong winds crashing against the ship from all sides. It was only at dawn, where Robinson Crusoe stepped out of his cabin on the shouts of "Land, land ho!" Even as Robinson Crusoe rushed towards the deck to see the signs of land himself, the ship suddenly sailed right into a dry sand tuft and came to a screeching halt.

Whatever measures the Captain and his men took to free the ship turned completely futile. The hurricane still lashed at the ship and Crusoe knew that it was only going to be a matter of time before the ship came apart completely. The Captain too realised this fact and having no other alternative before him, he called on the crew to abandon ship.

The crew members at once got busy lowering the only lifeboat that was present on board. As soon as it hit the water, everyone quickly climbed in. The wind was a bit more gentle at that time, but the ocean waves were still rowdy and dangerous. The boat naturally had no sail, and therefore, the crew were not able to row it and were dragged about in all directions by the furious sea.

And in that darkness, no one noticed a large wave come from behind. It was almost thirty feet high and as it came crashing over the lifeboat, no one stood a chance as the entire lifeboat capsized, taking all eleven members down with it.

Robinson Crusoe tried desperately to swim to safety at first. However, his expert swimming capabilities were no match for the raging waves of the ocean and he could feel himself sink under

the pressure of the water. He could not fight against the force of the sea any longer and felt himself being carried away by the sea before his consciousness started to fade.

Suddenly, a huge wave dragged him out of the water and took him forward with great force. Crusoe was certain that the wave would throw him so far deep into the sea that he would surely not be able to resurface in time and would die. However, when the wave crashed through, he fell flat on a hard surface. Even though he was quite badly hurt, Crusoe tried to raise his head and see where he was.

He could not see very clearly in the darkness, but he could make out that he was on some kind of land. As the next wave hit the shore and tried to drag him back into the sea, Crusoe dug his hands and feet into the soft sand and managed to claw his way inwards.

As he tried to get up and run deeper into the land, a wave came crashing in and pushed him

forward, making him crash into a large rock. Crusoe groaned in pain as the rock hit him hard on the face, but he realised that he would have to move fast, before the next wave took him back in again.

Gathering all the strength that he had left in him, Crusoe managed to get up on his feet and started running further away from the shore. As soon as he was certain that he was far away from the reach of the waves, he simply fell down on the sand, unconscious.

It was a little while after Robinson Crusoe finally managed to come around. As soon as he opened his eyes, he started coughing, and then vomiting the sea water that he had consumed while swimming towards the shore. As he pulled himself up, the first thing he did was say a prayer of thanks to the Almighty — after all, he was the only member of the ship who had survived. Everyone else who had climbed into the lifeboat with him had died in the hurricane.

As he walked along the shoreline, Crusoe could see the wreckage of his dilapidated ship. As it was still quite a long distance away from the shore, Crusoe realised that it was a miracle that he had managed to find his way to the shoreline where he was now standing.

However, as he slowly came around to his surroundings, Robinson Crusoe's joy of surviving the hurricane gave way to fear. He was certain that he was alone, but who knew where he was? His first thought was about food and water. Did he manage to survive that ferocious hurricane, only to die of hunger and thirst? Or would he die fighting some wild beast on the island? And even worse, he realised that he wouldn't even be able to fight any animal since he had no weapons or instruments to defend himself with.

He was so scared of the possibilities of death that now lay in store for him, that he started thumping his breast and screamed, "What kind of an evil joke is this? I was saved only to die a more horrendous death!"

Crusoe realised that he would have to make himself stronger. He quickly started walking deeper into the island, and soon he came upon a little stream. He drank that water and quenched his thirst.

Crusoe was hungry, but he consoled himself by thanking his stars that he was still alive to begin with. He then set off looking for a place to sleep that night. He found a large tree and quickly climbed up on to one of the branches there. This would perhaps be the best place for him to spend the night safe from any wild animals.

Looking up at the night sky and the stars, fearing for his life, Crusoe soon passed into deep sleep.

Chapter Three

A New Beginning

It was a bright sunny day when Robinson Crusoe woke up the next morning. The skies were clear, and the storm had all but passed away. Crusoe instinctively pushed apart the thick bushy branches on the tree he was sleeping on to take a good look at the now sombre sea. He could see his wrecked vessel, now free from the sand tuft it had gotten stuck in the night before, had now been brought closer to the seashore with the tide.

Crusoe looked on at the ship and thought about his ill-fortuned crew members. "Poor

souls! Had they not left the ship to begin with, all of them would have been alive right now."

However, Crusoe soon realised that he couldn't waste any more time in lamenting the dead. He decided to go back out to the sea at once and try and get on board the ship. His first task would be to bring back any goods and commodities that he could salvage from the ship. They would perhaps come of invaluable use to him.

By the time the sun reached directly overhead, the tide had almost gone completely back to the deep sea and it was easy enough for Robinson Crusoe to swim out to the sea. He found a rope hanging from the ship and quickly climbed up through it and reached the deck.

His good fortune was still smiling on him as all the food that had been taken as provisions during the journey was intact and unspoiled by the sea water. Seeing all that food lying before him, his hunger came back to him and he started stuffing as many biscuits in his mouth as he could. As he then started to put more and more biscuits into the pockets of his worn out coat, he realised that he would need to take back a lot more with him from the ship than just food. And therefore, it was evident that he needed a boat.

He moved around through the deck and found some broken masts lying there. Tying a piece of rope to each log, he pushed them overboard into the water, holding the rope securely so that the log pieces did not float away. He then climbed down the rope once again and started tying all the logs together, making a raft for himself.

It was quite some time since then that Robinson Crusoe was able to fill his raft with all kinds of provisions. He took with him all the loose boards that he could find on the ship. He then filled an empty chest with all the food that was there on the ship, and even took several bottles of rum with him. He even took his clothes, since the ones he was wearing were in complete rags because of the rough incident he had had in the sea.

He also found the entire load of tools on board the ship, like saws, axes, hammers and nails and he took them down to his raft as well. And finally, he took with him the entire stash of arms and ammunitions that were on board the ship. He found a few good shotguns, a couple of pistols and even a sword, which had already started to rust. He knew these would be necessary for him to start life all over again on the island, particularly if he were attacked by some aboriginal natives or wild animals.

Just as he was ready to set sail for the island once again, the tide started to rush in towards the land once again. This helped him move his raft with considerable ease. However, as he came closer to the sea shore, a strong current started taking him away from where he had first come into the water on his way to the ship earlier.

Crusoe had sailed on many voyages to know that the current necessarily indicated towards the presence of some inland creek or river. This was indeed a good sign for Crusoe, as it would be much easier for him to take his raft to the banks of a creek, than try and push it up through the sandy sea shore.

And it turned out, he was indeed right. For in a short while he could spot the creek and could see how the current was dragging him towards it. Just as he entered the creek, Crusoe spotted a little cove on the banks of the creek. He quickly gauged that the cove would be ideal for him to bring in his raft, and moreover, it wasn't that far from the sea either — so he could watch out for ships from there and hopefully be rescued from the island.

As he tied his raft to a thick huge tree in the cove, Robinson Crusoe realised that he would first have to get a better idea about the environment that he was in. He needed to establish whether he was on an island, or was this the edge of a mainland. He therefore, set off along a steep hill next to the cove, so that he could get an aerial view of his surroundings.

As he reached the summit of the hill, he looked around and saw the sea in every direction. Clearly he was marooned on an island. He then returned to where he had left his raft and quickly got to work building a small hut for himself with all the loose boards that he had brought back from the ship. Once it was ready, Crusoe decided to take some rest.

However, he realised that he would have to plan his next course of action on the seemingly uninhabited island. His first task was to go back to the ship and bring back as much goods and equipment that he could salvage. His fear was that in the event of another hurricane, the ship would surely be smashed to smithereens and then everything would be lost to him forever.

Therefore, he got back on the raft and set off for the ship once again. He decided to make as many trips as required to the ship, before he could take some well-deserved rest.

The next three weeks passed in Crusoe's going to the ship and coming back with more and more goods. He brought back every single tool that he could find on the ship and also found himself a compass, a spyglass along with some clothes, blankets, ropes and maps. He even found some gold and silver coins and even though they would have no value on the island, he decided to take them along too. And finally, he brought back with him his only four companions on the island — the dog that had been a part of the ship's company, two cats and a copy of the Bible.

Robinson Crusoe had indeed been right in deciding to make as many trips as possible to the ship, since the fourth week of his stay saw the outbreak of a violent storm. When he awoke the next morning, Crusoe saw that the ship had completely vanished from his line of sight. Later, he saw the debris of the ship being washed up along the sea shore.

His first priority therefore was to build a hut for himself. And he also wanted to find a location that could be easily seen from the sea, since he still nursed hopes of being rescued by a passing ship one day.

And thus began a new life for Robinson Crusoe on that unknown island. It was difficult for him to record the days he spent there, particularly since he did not have any paper or pens to make a note. Taking a large log, Crusoe planted it into the ground and for each day that he spent on the island, he would scratch a notch into it. After seven such notches marked seven days, Crusoe would make a longer slash across the seven notches, marking a week spent on the island. A week then turned into a month, and a month into a year.

Chapter Four

Learning New Things

It was after many days that Robinson Crusoe finally found a small little plain land along the side of a hill. It was the ideal location where Crusoe built his hut. Moreover, a portion of the hill had been washed away, making the portion look like an opening to a cave. Crusoe quickly got to work and built his hut in that opening.

He took some of the sails that he brought back from the sinking ship and placed them around the opening, making a cozy place for him to sit and sleep in. More importantly, he chopped down some young strong trees and made them into small stumps with pointed ends. These he then planted all along the ground, from one end of the hill to another. Now this fence created a fortress, protecting him, his house and all his belongings from the rest of the island. To get in or out of the fortress, Crusoe made a ladder which he pulled in with himself when he went back inside.

Once the hut and the surrounding protection was done, Crusoe got busy digging against the side of the hill. He needed a cool space where he could store all his provisions and the side of the hill within his little fortress. They would be untouched by rain or the sun and would remain safe for quite some time.

However, Crusoe was a clever man and he knew that would not be able to survive just on the goods that he had brought back from the ship. He therefore, went hunting each and every day, coming back with the game he managed to hunt — he found pigeons, goats, turtles, ducks, everything that he needed to survive on the

island. The goat's milk soon became his staple diet, along with the turtle eggs that he managed to get for himself. There was also one time, when he hunted an animal he had never see before in his life. But the animal's meat wasn't eatable one bit. Crusoe therefore, skinned the animal's hide and made clothes for himself out of it.

Now that the hut was ready and he had established a kind of food chain for himself, Robinson Crusoe decided to turn his attention to furnishing his house. He had never done much work with tools before, and it took him quite some many attempts with the axe and the saw, before he made himself some tables, chairs and shelves.

Robinson Crusoe also realised that since he had such a lot of free time on the island, he needed to do something to keep himself busy. One day, he found the sacks of barleycorn that he had brought back from the ship, and decided to try his hand at farming.

He searched around the island, and found a flat plain land close to his hut. There he started to dig up the entire land at his disposal and ploughed it as well. Of course, he faced several difficulties — the most important one being that he did not have a spade with him. He therefore, had to use hardwood trees and even though it took a lot of hard work, he finally managed to make himself a wooden spade which worked just wonderfully in digging up the soil.

However, Crusoe later realised that he had sowed his crops in the wrong season. Naturally, his farming came to nothing that time. But when he later sowed the remaining half of the seeds before the monsoons, his crops grew just fine.

As the crops grew, Crusoe made it a point to save all the ripe corn as and when they were ready to be plucked. It was by replanting the ripe corn labouriously, year after year, that he was able to increase the size of his farm and then make his first bread on the island, three years from the time he sowed his first successful crop.

With the passage of time, Robinson Crusoe decided to travel along the creek to the interior portions of the island. Therefore, it was after a good ten months that he first came along fields of naturally grown wild tobacco and sugar canes, and a lot of fruit trees, like grapes, oranges and lemons. Crusoe had to consume the fruits as soon as he plucked them from the trees — all except the grapes, since he could store them till they became resins. These fruits helped him to fight against starvation on the island.

And because he could store the grapes, it became all the more valuable to him during the monsoons. He couldn't venture far into the island during the rains, where the fruit trees grew and it was only with great difficulty that he managed to hunt a deer or two during such times. The dried resins however, kept him in good steed during this bleak period.

By the time he completed one whole year living on the island, Robinson Crusoe knew the pattern

of seasons on the island. This was particularly beneficial to him for the purpose of farming. He managed to divide the year into periods of dry, rain, dry and rain, quite unlike what it used to be in England. Moreover, such knowledge also helped in storing provisions.

He spent quite a lot of time in digging around the cave, increasing its depth so as to increase the area of his own dwelling. He also made several baskets with the help of the long twigs that were lying in abundance around the entire island. These baskets helped him in storing corns and resins and also in collecting dirt and rocks that accumulated as a result of his indoors expansion.

With the advent of the second year on the deserted island, Crusoe made several excursions to the deep interior of his new home. On one fine day, he even managed to reach the peak of the highest hill on the island and he looked carefully in all directions. He spied land nearly forty miles to the west, but he wasn't sure whether that

land was part of another island or whether it belonged to some mainland. However, he had no intentions of going that far to find out, because he was certain that if people lived in those parts, then clearly they were uncivilized savages. He had heard many tales of cannibals in this region, people who ate other people, during his stay in Brazil and he was grateful that he had landed on the island than amidst a group of hungry cannibals.

Once during his many trips, Robinson Crusoe landed amidst a flock of parrots. He even managed to bring back one parrot to his cave, and after four years of training, the parrot was finally able to say, "Robin Crusoe!"

And with the end of the second year of exile on that deserted island, began the third year of Robinson Crusoe's adventures. By now his crops had grown so much that he did not need to replant any more corn to expand his farmland. Crusoe decided that it was now time for him to

make bread. But that was easier said than done, since he would now need a mill to grind the ripe corn, a sieve to strain it, jars to store it in and finally, an oven to bake the bread in.

His first attempt at making clay jars that he formed by mixing clay and water turned to be completely futile. The ugly looking paste jars that he tried to dry in the sun either cracked at once, or they crumbled to the ground when he tried to hold them in his hand.

It was after two whole months that he finally succeeded in making the right mixture to make himself some earthen bowls, dishes and pots. He even tried to make two large pots, if one could call them that, but they turned out to be too ugly to even use properly.

However, he quickly moved to his next objective and that was to find a stone to grind his corn with. The stones that were available on the island could not take the pounding required and turned to dust in no time. Crusoe therefore,

used the hardwood trees to fashion a pestle and mortar.

The next step was to separate the husk from the meal that he made after grinding the corns. But he didn't have a sieve or muslin cloth. He remembered however, taking a neckerchief from the ship on one his trips to the sinking vessel. Removing some threads from the neckerchief, he was able to fashion out a sieve for himself.

Robinson's mind had developed quite a lot since he started living on the island and he immediately came up with an ingenuous solution to his oven problem as well. He put his dough into one earthen pot and covered it with another on top of it. He then placed the pot filled with dough on red-hot coals and then poured more coals over the covered pot. Sure enough, the coals started to bake the bread! Three years at the island had taught Robinson a huge lot.

Chapter Five

A Canoe

It was almost four years since the time Robinson Crusoe first landed on the island that he was to call his home. And in those four years, he often wondered about the tract of land he had seen that day from atop the tallest hill on the island.

Now that he had mastered the elements and also managed to make his life seemingly comfortable on the island, Crusoe decided to finally make an attempt to travel to that distance piece of land towards the western shore and see if there was some way he could plan his escape.

He realised that the easiest and the fastest way for him to get across would be to make a canoe.

He remembered the natives in Brazil making such canoes from tree trunks and he decided to make one for himself.

He chose a thick cedar tree, which was nearly six feet long and heavy enough to be turned into a canoe. Cutting it down to the ground alone took him a week and he spent another two weeks in clearing away all its branches. The next month was spent in cutting and chiseling away at the bottom end of the trunk, so as to make it floatable. And finally, Robinson Crusoe spent close to three months in clearing the insides of the trunk, so as to make it a proper canoe.

Five months later, Robinson Crusoe's efforts had finally turned successful. His magnificent canoe was now ready to sail. However, it was only then that Crusoe faced his biggest problem yet with the canoe — and that was dragging it to the water. The boat was big and heavy enough to carry a load of twenty people, and therefore it was nearly impossible to drag to the inland creek, which was at least a hundred yards away from where the canoe was being made.

However much he tried, the canoe did not budge even an inch. And therefore, Crusoe had to finally abandon all hopes of ever seeing that canoe sailing. Five months of his life were completely wasted, except that it taught him one important lesson for the future — that he always needed to plan ahead for such cases. Whenever he would get around to making another boat, he would have to make sure that his new canoe was lighter and also that he would have to construct it on the banks of the creek.

Since he had some time on his hands now before starting work on the second canoe, Robinson Crusoe decided to do something about the clothes that he had on the island. For all of the four years that he had now spent on the island, Crusoe had been wearing the same clothes that he had managed to bring back with himself from the ship. Naturally, they now just hung on his

body in rags. It was true that the weather was quite hot in the region and there was no soul in sight, yet clothes were necessary to shield himself from the blaring sun that often resulted in terrible headaches for the marooned traveller.

Since he wanted to make new clothes for himself, Crusoe first started going through all the fabric that he had at his disposal. He took all the animal skins that he had taken off the animals he had hunted and dried them all in the sun. The soft ones, like the goat skins, seemed to be easy enough to sew into new clothes for himself.

He first fashioned a cap for himself, one which had a flap running down the nape of his neck. The fur on the flap was a welcome relief during the monsoons and also acted as a guard against the sun.

Since the cap turned out to be prett Robinson Crusoe then got busy the clothes to wear around his bo

the same kinds of goat skin to make himself a loose waistcoat and also a kind of vest. He made pants too with the goat skin and also a belt. He made several little slots in the belt, allowing him to carry his axe and his hatchet easily. And he then made another belt which he used to hang over his shoulder. This could hold his small pouches of gunpowder, thus proving to be quite useful when Crusoe would go out hunting. Finally, he made himself a pair of shoes, which quite honestly looked like socks.

Robinson Crusoe was extremely proud of the clothes that he had managed to sew. This had been the first attempt in his entire life at tailoring, and like everything else, he had excelled in this department too. When he put on his entire outfit for the first time, he did look kind of scary. But of course, he was completely alone on the island and therefore, he succeeded at terri

Robinson Crusoe now became ambitious and proud of his work o₁ he now set off trying to make an umbrella, which would come of great use to him both during the monsoons, and when the sun was breathing fire down on him. Making an umbrella wasn't as easy as making clothes, and it took him nearly three to four times to come up with something that resembled an umbrella. However, he managed to do a good job with the goat skin and the branches of a tree, and the umbrella could be opened and closed at his will — something that turned out to be quite effective for him to carry around.

It was only at the close of the fifth year of his living at the island that Robinson Crusoe decided to take another attempt at making a canoe. He kept in mind the reason for his failure from the first attempt and got to work at once.

The second time the canoe was small and Crusoe had no trouble at all in pushing it out to the water. However, unlike last time, this canoe was too small to wade across the sea to the new ıd that he had spied from atop the tall hill.

Crusoe therefore, decided to take a tour around his own island in his new canoe.

To help him get along faster, Crusoe adjusted a mast to his canoe and made a sail out of the little pieces of the sails that he had brought back with himself from the ship. Not knowing how long a trip around the island would take, Crusoe also built a small little safe along the side of the canoe, in which he stored some provisions like food, one gun and also some gunpowder. He also took his umbrella and fixed it to the rear end of the canoe, allowing him to sit in the shade as he steered his canoe around the island.

For the first few months, Robinson Crusoe sailed his canoe in the creek alone, mastering its ways and methods. At the beginning of his sixth year on the island, Crusoe finally decided to attempt sailing the seas for the first time. He directed his canoe eastwards, towa rock that edged out almost six miles i Once he reached across the rock, he s coast extending nearly three miles out to the sea, before it went into some more rocks at the edge. Robinson Crusoe would now have to sail nine miles into the sea, before he could banks inwards to the coast once again. And this canoe wasn't big or strong enough for him to take that risk easily.

Therefore, Crusoe first pulled into the rocks at the end of the sand coast and tied his canoe there. He then quickly made his way along the coast to a hill nearby and reaching the summit, he looked out through his spyglass and first studied the terrain that he was in. He noticed a terrible current flowing along the other side of the rocks, and it dawned on him that sailing along the sand bar would most probably take him into the current, and therefore far away into sea. And his canoe would surely not be able to take the rough choppy sea waves and crumble at once.

However, there was also no other way for Crusoe to progress, and therefore, he decided to take his chances against the current, irrespective of the odds.

What seemed to be just impossible, soon turned out to be more than just fatal. Robinson Crusoe tried to muster all his strength in maneuvering his canoe along the side of the current, but it just seemed to be of no avail. For more than five hours he paddled as hard and quick as he could, but nothing seemed to be working for the poor sailor. Fortunately, a strong gust of wind blew him along the side of the current and he was saved from a certain death. However, he was still not in a much better position than he was earlier, as now he was completely lost. The breeze had no doubt pushed him away from the current, but where exactly had it taken him? Crusoe first made a pledge with himself — that in the event he survived this incident, he would henceforth make sure that he always carried his compass with him on these voyages.

Then, seeing that the wind was actually picking up, Crusoe pulled out the sail and

drifted along the low sea waves, till he finally reached the northern bank of the island.

After resting a while, he decided to go back to his side of the island. But the experience of sailing through that life threatening current once was more than what Crusoe was willing to gamble and therefore, he set off trying to find an alternate route back to his fortress, and decided to complete his mission on foot. He tied his canoe securely to the large trees at the edge of the island and with a heavy heart, he set off for home. It would be another few months before he would get another canoe ready to sail in.

Chapter Six

Someone Else?

Another five years had been completed by Robinson Crusoe on the deserted island that had now become his new home. The resources, like gunpowder, that he had managed to score off the ship before it sank, were now starting to dwindle. And the point was that without any gunpowder it would became absolutely impossible for Crusoe to hunt for food anymore.

He therefore, started using more ingenuous methods to catch his prey from then on. For instance, the first trap that he managed to set actually fetched him three goats. One of them was a male and the other two were femal

Instead of using them as meat for his food, Crusoe instead started rearing them and within the next year and a half, he had twelve goats with him. By two years' time since then, Robinson Crusoe's fortress held more than forty goats.

Crusoe then started to use the goat flock that he had to supply him with milk, as well as meat for his meals. Milking goats was an entirely new experience for Robinson Crusoe — but as with all his other experiments on the island, he achieved success after the first few attempts. Soon he started to make cheese and butter as well.

One day, as he struck another notch against his log calendar, Crusoe realised that he had spent more than seven years on the island, since his not so successful visit to the northern end of the island. Unable to live a life of stagnation any more, Robinson Crusoe decided to go back to the northern bank and bring back his canoe. At least then he would be able to move about more freely than usual.

Since he had not built another sailing vessel since that last canoe, Crusoe had to walk back towards the northern edge. After many hours, when he could spot the northern edge in his sight, he looked around and saw that the sea had completely died down. The current which had almost taken his life was gone. Crusoe tried to understand the reason behind this awkward phenomena and then it struck him — it was the low tide! Crusoe therefore, decided to make haste and reach his canoe, so that he could use the low tide to his advantage and sail out from there.

As he increased his speed and made haste for the canoe, Crusoe's eyes fell on something unique. It startled him so badly that Robinson Crusoe just froze in his tracks. Clearly marked in the ground before him were a trail of footprints! Robinson Crusoe first kept standing there for what seemed to be an eternity. Then very carefully, he knelt before the footprints and studied them carefully. There was no doubt in his mind that the footprints were those of a man — it had five toes, a heel, everything. And he measured it against his own feet. Clearly they belonged to some other man since the prints were bigger than those created by his own feet.

On his first instinct, Crusoe ran around the area, desperately trying to catch a glimpse of that someone, or even hear some sound that would lead him to the other man on the island. He then ran up the hill and looked out in all directions, yet nothing. He came running down and started running along the shore once again, trying very hard to spot someone who could have made those footprints.

The suspense finally got the better of him, and without giving any more thought to retrieving his canoe, Robinson Crusoe started running back towards his home. He was crippled with fear all through the way back home, turning back at every step to see whether he was being

followed or not. He finally managed to find some peace when he was secure inside his fortress much later.

As much as he tried, Robinson Crusoe could get no sleep that night. He kept tossing and turning in his bed all night, seeing those footprints float before his very eyes. Surely he had not seen any boat in the vicinity and neither had there been any more than that single set of footprints. Then who could be there on that island with him?

And even as he tried to reason with himself, another more terrifying thought got his fancy completely. He started imagining a group of savages caught in that current by the northern edge, who having landed there from the mainland had found his canoe and were now looking to kill him and eat him!

Crusoe did not leave the safety and security of his fortress for the next few days. It was only after pondering over the issue for the next three to four days, that he finally manage to find his

courage again. He reasoned with himself that in his fifteen years on the island, he had never seen a living soul. In which case, was the footprint really that worrying?

Robinson Crusoe started to believe in his own argument. Yet, he did not want to take any chances against the bearer of that mysterious footprint. He spent the next few days fortifying his house further. He added another rung of stakes around the ones that he already had and he placed the muskets he had brought back from the ship in strategic cracks in the wall.

But even a whole month's hard work and a second wall did not give Robinson Crusoe much peace. After all, how was he to know if there really were savages there on the island?

Chapter Seven

Man Eaters!

Robinson Crusoe had mustered enough courage to roam about near his fortress, hunting for food and collecting the fruits that grew around his house. But in those two years that he spent on the island since, not for once did he dare venture towards the eastern edge of the island, to the place where he had spotted that mysterious footprint.

However, that did not stop him from paying a visit to the western end of the island. As he arrived at the western edge, he carried out his usual practice of climbing the tallest hill there and taking a look around the portion of the island. As

he stared out towards the sea, Crusoe felt that he spotted something that looked like a boat — but since he did not have his spyglass with him, there was no way for him to be absolutely sure about what he had seen. As he stared on at that boat like object, it soon sailed out of his line of sight.

Crusoe turned his attention away from the object that he had seen in the waters and started climbing down the hill again, so as to resume his journey. But just as he reached the bottom of the hill, all that he could do was just stand there and stare in horror.

Before him lay an entire pile of human bones. There were skulls, hands, feet, entire skeletons lying before him. A terrified Crusoe looked around him to see a fire still burning beside the skeleton pile.

"Cannibals... this has got to be the work of cannibals," Crusoe said to himself, shivering in fear. Crusoe could not look at the carnage in front of him any longer. Unable to control himself, he started to vomit just thinking about the cannibals at their work.

After having recovered slightly, Robinson Crusoe started running back from the western end of the island, and did not stop till he was safely within his fortress. His mind was made up — he would never again travel to the western edge of the island.

From that day onwards, to the next two years that he actually spent on the island, Robinson Crusoe seldom left the confines of his fortress. He even stopped firing his gun to hunt animals, lest that attract the savages to his presence. Instead he continued feed on the goats that he had reared. However, Robinson Crusoe always kept his gun, along with some more pistols and his sword, just in case the savages and his paths crossed ever in the future.

However, staying locked up inside the fortress just turned Robinson Crusoe's mind to anger and frustration. He started thinking of ways in which

he could lay siege to the savages and kill them before they got to him. Nothing seemed viable enough for him though, considering he was just one man against a gang of twenty savages at the least. His weapons too would be no match for their ingenuous ammunition and he would certainly not win in such a situation. Yet, Crusoe believed that he needed to do something before the savages got to him.

And as he thought more and more about the cannibals, he started to question and reason with himself about their nature. "Who am I to think ill about these men? I certainly do not think it wrong to kill and eat goats... perhaps they too think the same about human beings. In which case, would it be right for me to kill them?"

"And then again," continued Crusoe, "This was their island to begin with. I came here later and started living here and now I am making them out to be the enemy. Moreover, I might even kill a couple of savages, but what if that

just infuriates them more and they come back to attack me with a couple of hundred of their tribesmen?" These questions haunted Robinson Crusoe for quite some many days.

Finally, Crusoe came to the conclusion that in the event he ever came before the cannibals during his stay on the island, he would merely hide and escape from them, instead of trying to get into a fight with them. It was better that they did not know about his presence on the island.

Life did become a lot harder for Robinson Crusoe on the island once he was aware of the presence of these cannibals. Every time he had to leave his fortress to go out just filled him with fear and worry. He even stopped making additions to his house, even at the cost of making life more comfortable for himself — after all, the savages would hear the sounds of his hammering and sawing and would perhaps come to find him. As for lighting fires in his fortress, Robinson Crusoe knew that his own personal safety came before anything else. He therefore, started cooking his goat meat inside the cave, so as to not give out a smoke trail to the cannibals.

It was now four years after that incident with the footprints and a total of twenty-three years that Crusoe had managed to stay on the island. Since the savages had never come before him in all those years, Crusoe slowly started to believe that perhaps their paths would never cross.

However, in December that very same year, something happened that proved to be contrary to Crusoe's new found belief. As he left his fortress that morning and started moving towards where the fruit trees grew, he spotted a smoke trail not very far from where he was.

Curious, Crusoe immediately climbed up a small little hill over his fortress and lying flat on his stomach, so as to not be seen by anyone, he directed his spyglass in the direction of the smoke trail. As was expected, he saw a group of nine cannibals sitting by the fire. He continued to

watch them, till they all went back to their canoes and sailed away from there.

Robinson waited for them to go away at first and then he quickly took his guns and started off for the beach. Once again, the same sight greeted him. There were all kinds of skeletal bones lying in the ground where the fire was burning. Clearly these savages were eating human beings once again. This ignited Robinson Crusoe once again and he made up his mind once and for all — the savages would not survive the next time they would come before Robinson Crusoe.

Chapter Eight

Precious Words

After living in peace for so many years on the island, the repeated incidents with the savages now turned Robinson Crusoe's mind towards escape. He could not stand the silence any longer. He wanted to talk to someone, or at least find someone who could get him out of this island and take him back to civilization.

Crusoe had seen a faint glimmer of hope a few years back, when a Spanish ship had floated around to the shores of the island. However, when Crusoe finally reached there, all he found were dead bodies aboard the vessel. He was

forced to return with whatever little cargo and supplies that were still left on the ship.

He had brought back with him some muskets, gunpowder and some clothes, all of which he was desperately in need of. Also, he found a pet dog aboard the ship and brought him back too. Now he would at least have someone to talk to, in whatever little way it was possible, since his first pet had died many years ago.

He had also come back with the bags of gold that he had found aboard the Spanish vessel. But for the first time in his life, all that gold had no effect on Crusoe. After all, what would he do with all that in his deserted island. He would have been much happier had he found a living human being.

Robinson Crusoe now had only one thing on his mind — his eventual escape from his adopted home, the island. He kept charting plans all through the day, and even at night his dreams were only centered around his escape. And every night, he started to see the same dream over and over again. He would see a prisoner, escaping from the savages and running towards him. Crusoe helped the man to safety and they started to live together in his fortress. His dreams showed how the native that he had managed to rescue would eventually help him in reaching civilization once again.

He kept seeing this dream so often that after some time, Crusoe started believing it to be some kind of a sign. He made up his mind to save one of the prisoners of the savages. He was sure that if he did so, the rest of his dream would also come true.

He quickly put his plan into action and therefore, he started watching the shoreline from a distance. But days turned into months, and moths into years — still there was no movement along the coast.

However, his luck changed on the twenty-fifth year of his stay on the island. One morning, he

found five canoes standing along the coastline. He was convinced that the savages had already reached, and judging by the number of canoes present there, Crusoe estimated that at least some twenty savages must have come to the island. Crusoe wondered whether it would be a wise decision for him to get into a fight with such a large number of savages!

Quickly climbing a hill, Robinson Crusoe looked out in every direction, till he saw a smoke trail rising from a distance. He could see around thirty cannibals dancing around a fire, even as some kind of meat cooked on the fire. Crusoe tried his level best to make out if the meat belonged to an animal or a human being, but he could not be sure.

He continued to keep watch, till he saw the savages starting to drag two natives that they had left tied in a canoe. Before his very eyes, he saw the cannibals grab one of the natives and after striking him unconscious first, they started to skin him like he was a wild animal.

As the cannibals were busy with their prey, the other native saw that he had been left completely unguarded and he started to run away from the cannibals, moving towards where Robinson Crusoe was standing.

Crusoe was completely shocked and surprised. It was just as he had witnessed in his dream. He looked carefully and saw the savages send three of their men after the fleeing native.

"This should not be too difficult now. As it is, the native seems to be way faster than the savages," thought Crusoe to himself. He kept silently praying for the native, hoping that he would make it out of there alive.

As the native arrived at the inland creek, Crusoe wondered, "I hope he can swim… else all will be lost! Those natives will kill him the moment they can get their hands on him."

Crusoe continued to watch in great excitement as the native plunged into the water without even stopping and in a few short strokes, made it to the other side of the creek. Two savages jumped after him and started swimming to the other side. The third savage gave up and started walking back towards where the rest of his tribesmen were.

Moreover, the savages that did know how to swim were not as good as the native and by the time they could cross the creek, the native had moved far away from their grasp.

Crusoe realised that it was now time for him to intervene and help that native get to safety. Getting off the hill as quickly as he could, Crusoe quickly left his fortress and started moving towards the creek.

As soon as he reached the creek, he saw the native run past him. Crusoe whistled, getting the native's attention in the process. He gestured towards the man to come towards him, but

the poor native was too close to his own death a few moments back and did not trust Robinson Crusoe.

Suddenly, Crusoe heard the sound of footsteps rushing towards where he was. He knew that the savages must have almost arrived to where he was standing. Not wanting to fire his gun and attract unnecessary attention to himself, Crusoe used the end of his gun to bash against the head of the first native.

However, the second native saw Robinson Crusoe attack his friend and he quickly drew on his bow and arrow to kill Crusoe. Crusoe realised that he wouldn't be able to get close enough to the second native in time to use the end of his gun, and therefore, he was forced to fire at his attacker.

The native, who saw Crusoe attack the two men who were following him, now froze in his tracks. The sound of the gun going off was too much for him to take.

Seeing the native standing and looking back towards him, Robinson Crusoe once again motioned towards the native to come closer to him. Frightened, the poor native started walking very slowly towards Crusoe. He would kneel down and stretch his arms towards Crusoe every ten steps. Robinson Crusoe thought that perhaps the native was trying to show his gratitude to Crusoe for taking care of his attackers.

Robinson Crusoe tried to make the native feel a little easier by smiling warmly at him. By the time the native was close enough, he immediately fell to the ground and started kissing the soil before Crusoe. Then, in a quick move, he lifted Crusoe's foot and placed it on his head. "Maybe he is trying to say that he shall be my slave forever," thought Crusoe to himself.

Crusoe immediately bent down towards the native and lifted him by his shoulders. He embraced the shocked native, making him feel safe. Just then the first savage whom Crusoe

had merely struck unconscious started to come around slowly.

The native pointed to Crusoe's sword and made a motion of killing the savage. Bewildered and amused at the same time, Crusoe took his sword and gave it to the native. The man did not even waste another moment as he rushed over to his attacker and drove the rusty blade right through him, killing the cannibal at once.

He returned to where Crusoe was standing and placed the sword respectfully at Crusoe's hide clad feet.

Now, they would first have to bury the two dead bodies, so that their tribesmen would not be able to find them easily.

As soon as the bodies were taken care of, Crusoe led the native back to his house. After giving the native some food to eat and some water to drink, Crusoe arranged for the native to sleep for a while.

Chapter Nine

A Friend

For quite some time, Crusoe just stood quietly over the sleeping native and stared at him. It had been twenty five years now since he was standing in the presence of another man. The native had rather exquisite features. He was tall and seemed to be quite strong. Crusoe estimated the young man to be around twenty-five years of age. Crusoe even carefully looked at the man's straight thick black hair that fell around his face as he slept.

Crusoe then got busy with his chores around the fortress. It was around thirty minutes or so,

when he was milking the goats, that the native came rushing in to find Crusoe. He once again knelt down on the floor and placed Crusoe's feet over his head. Crusoe was now certain that the man was pledging his loyalty and gratitude to him for having saved him and brought him back to the fortress.

Crusoe decided to name the native 'Friday', since according to his log calendar, it was on a Friday that he had found the native, his new friend, his new companion.

Slowly, Crusoe started to educate Friday in the English language. It appeared that Friday was a good student, for that night itself, the young man learnt how to address Robinson Crusoe as his 'master', and by the next morning, he knew how and when to say 'yes' or 'no'.

Robinson Crusoe knew that he would have to keep a good watch out for the cannibals. The next day, both Crusoe and Friday went up the hill behind the fortress to see if they could spot the savages. But they looked in every direction and could not find anyone. Even the canoes were missing. Clearly the savages had gone back to wherever they lived, without even bothering to look for their missing friends.

As they walked back to the part of the island where they had buried the two dead cannibals, Friday made a gesture to Robinson Crusoe that they should dig up the bodies of the cannibals and eat them. Crusoe's stomach churned on seeing Friday make those signs, and he almost started to vomit. He realised at once that he would have to change Friday's habits from the cannibalism that he shared with his people.

He led the native to the part of the beach where the cannibals had gathered the day before. Crusoe immediately burnt all the remains that the savages had left behind.

The next few days were spent in great comfort and joy with Friday. There seemed to be a father-son equation between Robinson Crusoe

and Friday and soon there was no doubt in Crusoe's mind about Friday's loyalty to him. He too started teaching Friday many things from western civilization, most importantly, the English language.

Friday too seemed to be quite intelligent and he devoted himself completely to Crusoe's lessons on English. He listened to his teacher intently and started picking up the language quite quickly.

A couple of years more were thus spent on the island in this fashion. Crusoe started to enjoy his life on the island now, what with Friday too living with him, serving him as a faithful servant and a true friend. The only thing that kept worrying Crusoe was an attack from the savages and that was the only reason why Crusoe wanted to still escape from the island.

With Friday learning to understand and speak a little bit of English, he was soon able to tell Crusoe many things that the sailor had always wanted to know. The island's geography was well known to Friday, who claimed to have come to the island for feasts and other such festivities many a time before. He readily explained all the currents and streams of the island, and made special mention of a particularly strong current that ran from the mainland towards the island. Crusoe was therefore soon able to understand that the island was situated at the mouth of the Orinoco River of South America, at the point where it ran into the Caribbean Sea.

Friday also told Robinson Crusoe everything about his race, his people, his country and also about the neighbouring lands. He also said, "West of here, there live white beard, master... he too look like you!"

This information allowed Crusoe to realise that Friday was surely talking of the Spaniards who had already established several colonies along various parts of South America. Knowing of where he was and who were his neighbours,

allowed Crusoe to start making realistic plans about his escape.

Crusoe needed to know how far these lands inhabited by the white men were, and when he asked Friday if there was some way in which they could reach these colonies, Friday replied, "We take canoe... we go!"

Robinson Crusoe understood that he would have to make a canoe that would be big enough to sail through rough waters and at the same time, it should be able to take both Crusoe and Friday.

Meanwhile, Robinson Crusoe and Friday continued to share more and more stories of their own people. Crusoe informed Friday about his life back in England and of how he had arrived on the island, and also of how he had started a new life there. He also spoke to him about the benefits of western civilization and also of their belief in God.

One day, Robinson Crusoe took Friday to the edge of the island where he had first landed

from the shipwreck. He showed him the broken remains of the lifeboat. On seeing the wreck, Friday at once said, "White men in this boat come to my home. We help white men arrive."

This information startled Crusoe and he excitedly asked, "White men? In your country? How many of them were there?"

Friday made some quick calculations with the help of his fingers and after much deliberation, he said, "Seven…teen white men!"

Now Crusoe was even more excited and he was hopeful, thinking that these men could perhaps include Crusoe in their group and together, they could perhaps find some means to escape back to the western world. "Where are they now?" Crusoe asked, hoping to hear a positive answer from Friday. The young native matter-of-factly replied, "They live with my people now."

Crusoe thought out loud to himself, "You say they came in a lifeboat like mine… clearly they

too must have been shipwrecked around these rocks here. And then the current from the Orinoco River must have dragged them over to the mainland, to your country."

On hearing Crusoe rambling on, Friday added, "White men like you living in my country total four years." Crusoe was a little astonished on hearing this and he asked, "And your people did not eat them up?"

"They like brothers of us," Friday explained. "And no eating man except when fighting war, that is the rule of my people. I fight war for our king, when I caught by evil men and brought to the island."

Crusoe was now quite hopeful of finding some of his own people in Friday's country and therefore, he asked the young native, "Would you like to go back home, to where your family is?"

Friday smiled and nodded, "I thank you for offer. I like to go back home."

Crusoe smiled on hearing Friday's honest answer and then he further asked, "And what will you do once you go back there? Eat human beings again like before?"

Friday seemed to be very hurt on hearing Crusoe speak that way. "Never! I never eat man meat again. I tell my people too of everything you teach men. We believe in God, we eat goat meat, and we drink goat milk. That is promise Friday makes to you."

Crusoe merely smiled at him and replied, "And will your people be pleased with that? Won't they kill you in anger?" Friday quickly replied, "My people wanting to learn. Like they learn from boat coming white men in my country."

Encouraged at Friday's words, Crusoe offered, "Then why don't you go back home?" Friday sadly shook his head and said, "Too far. Not able to swim that much."

Crusoe shrugged his shoulders and replied, "Don't worry about that. I'll make you a nice little

canoe." On hearing this, Friday's mood perked up once again and he replied, "Then I go. But master come with me, only then I go."

Crusoe smiled at Friday's innocent words and said, "Are you crazy? If I go there with you, your people will kill me and eat me up!"

Friday desperately flared his hands before Robinson Crusoe and said, "No, never, no… they not eat master. After all, master save my life. I tell them about everything that master done for me. They love you very much."

Assured by Friday's kindness, Crusoe took Friday to the other side of the island, where his second canoe still lay tied to the trees. Friday inspected the canoe carefully and declared, "Not going in this canoe. Canoe not able to go to my country. Too small canoe."

Crusoe immediately remembered his first canoe, the huge boat that could take nearly twenty people, but could not be taken to the sea because it was too big. But when he showed that

to Friday, the native started shaking his head once again and declared, "Canoe big, but canoe not sail. Canoe useless."

Crusoe smiled at Friday and soon, they started work on a new canoe. This one was big and sturdy and it was ready in a month.

Finally, when the rudder was fixed to the canoe, the two of them started sailing the waters on their new canoe.

As the canoe sailed out, for the first time in twenty-seven years, Robinson Crusoe felt the glowing hope of escape from the island rise in him. Hopefully, his log calendar would not have to see the marks of another year on it.

Chapter Ten

Finding the Cannibals Again

By the time the canoe was ready to make the voyage to Friday's country on the mainland, monsoons had arrived on Robinson Crusoe's little island. Therefore, Crusoe and Friday decided to wait for a couple of months, before they could make their journey.

Instead, they decided to use that time to make the necessary preparations for their journey. Crusoe had no idea how long it would take for them to make the distance to Friday's country and therefore, it was essential that they were well stocked with food and other such requirements for the journey. Bread, meat, grapes, ammunition, everything was gathered and made ready for their trip.

However, as Crusoe was going around completing the little tasks that he had on hand one day, Friday came running to him within the fortress. He was completely out of breath, as he mumbled, "Master, danger... bad danger!"

Crusoe was alarmed on seeing the state Friday was in. As he pressed further, Friday managed to say, "Three canoe come to beach. Friday gone. Friday to be eaten by them." And he waved frantically in the direction where Crusoe had rescued Friday from the savages.

Crusoe did not panic and instead replied, "Be brave, my friend. You and I will take on these savages together. I will look after you and you will look after me in this battle. Are you with me?"

Friday received some confidence from the way in which Crusoe spoke to him and said, "I die if you tell me to, fight is easy!"

Crusoe quickly ran up the hill behind the fortress and directed his spyglass towards the beach. Friday was indeed right. Around twenty savages were walking along the thicket by the beach and it seemed to Crusoe that they had three prisoners with them.

Crusoe had seen enough. It was time to deal with these savages directly. Running back to his fortress, Crusoe gathered his guns, muskets, pistols and even grabbed his sword. Then turning to Friday, he said, "Here, take this with you..." as he handed over some guns and muskets to his companion. "Follow me carefully, and don't do anything until and unless I tell you to."

They quickly reached the edge of the beach and took cover behind some of the large trees there. The cannibals were seated in a large circle around the fire and it seemed that they were already eating one of the prey. The other two men were sitting beside them, all tied up.

Friday nudged Crusoe and pointing in the direction of the prisoners, he said, "Master,

white man, white man. He come to my country in boat." Crusoe confirmed with the help of his spyglass that their prisoner was indeed a white man.

Robinson Crusoe knew that at whatever cost, he would have to save the white man. As they slowly edged closer towards the group of savages, he knew that they did not have much time. A couple of cannibals had already started walking towards where the white man was tied. It seemed that he was going to be killed and eaten next.

Turning to Friday, Crusoe whispered, "Follow me and attack when I fire my first shot."

Robinson Crusoe very carefully took aim and fired his musket. One of the savages fell down dead, while two others were fatally wounded. Friday too fired his gun and got better results, shooting down two cannibals and injuring three.

The other savages who were still gathered there quickly got up and started looking around, frightened to their very core. They had no idea where the bullets had come from, and they did not know whether they should run or try and fight the attackers.

Crusoe then picked up his shotgun, which Friday did as well. Loading their guns with small pistol bullets which flew in every direction when fired, the two men fired once again. This time they killed two of the savages, but because of the nature of the bullets, they wounded many more cannibals in that one attempt.

The savages were now all covered in blood and were running frantically in every direction. Crusoe motioned to Friday to follow him, and picking up their muskets they now came out into the flat land. The savages, on finally seeing Crusoe and Friday, slumped to their feet. Even as a few of them tried to run, Friday's accurate fire killed all of them.

Crusoe, meanwhile, went over to the white prisoner and cut open his binding ropes with his

knife. The man was still extremely frightened and even though Crusoe asked him a few questions in Portuguese, the man just could not seem to answer. Crusoe drew out his flask of rum and offered the man some of it, so that he could regain his courage and steady his nerves.

As the man calmed down a bit, he turned to Robinson Crusoe and said, "Española". Crusoe understood at once that the man was indeed a Spaniard and he quickly explained to him, in broken Spanish, that they would need his help in fighting the rest of the savages.

The Spaniard grabbed a pistol and the sword and with renewed vigour, he chased after the savages. Within moments, he had killed two of them with his sword alone. However, a huge savage came and started fighting the Spaniard with his large wooden sword. Crusoe saw the Spaniard tackle the savage courageously, and even though he cut the savage twice on his face, the big native managed to throw the Spaniard down and tried to take his sword away.

Crusoe at once started to run in that direction, but even before he could get there, the Spaniard deftly brought his pistol out from his belt and killed the savage in one clean shot.

The few remaining cannibals were paddling away from there in their canoe. Friday however, did not seem to stop, and started running after them into the water, screaming, "We kill them, we kill them. They go back, they come with more."

Crusoe realised that Friday was indeed speaking the truth and he quickly set off towards the canoe, so as to chase after the savages and kill them. "Friday, come on… we need to finish them off quickly!"

But Friday was now standing still and staring at the third prisoner!

Chapter Eleven

More People

Robinson Crusoe did not understand the first few words that Friday screamed out on seeing the third prisoner, for he was speaking in his own native tongue. It seemed to Crusoe that the prisoner too was very excited on seeing Friday before him.

Turning to Crusoe, an ecstatic Friday yelled, "Father, my father!" The poor old man was still trembling, as he was of the belief that this was going to be his last day on earth. Crusoe immediately rushed over to him, even as Friday started to massage the old man's hands and legs, to revive his blood circulation.

Crusoe took out his bottle of rum, which Friday gently pressed to the old man's lips. He also fed his father some raisins, so that the old man could get his strength back.

However, in the entire euphoria of Friday finding his father, both Crusoe and he had lost track of the escaping savages. By the time they got back to the beach, the canoe was gone.

Robinson Crusoe and Friday then helped the wounded Spaniard to his feet and brought him where Friday's father was already resting. They helped the two men into one of canoes that belonged to the savages and quickly, they started to sail back towards their fortress. They pulled into the creek and as they arrived before their house, they managed to take the canoe into the bank, where they tied it to a tree.

The Spaniard and the old man were both taken indoors and were made to sit in the shade, as both Robinson Crusoe and Friday gave them something to eat and drink.

As the four men sat down, they started to talk. Friday was instrumental in translating all that Robinson Crusoe was saying into his native tongue, so that his father and the Spaniard could both follow with ease. The Spaniard had been living with the natives for quite some time now, and therefore he knew the native tongue well enough.

Their first concern was about the savages who had managed to escape. Friday's father was of the opinion that a storm was brewing and the savages would surely meet their end in that small canoe. The Spaniard added that even if they survived the storm, they would surely be blown away and would take many days to come back to their village.

Friday summed it up, saying that the four were probably very shaken by all that had happened. They would think that some evil spirits were after them and therefore, there were hardly any chances of them coming back to the island, ever.

This was confirmed by Friday's father, who claimed that the savages were muttering about spirits all through — after all, they couldn't believe that someone could kill from such a distance and that too shoot fire of all things.

When the Spaniard and Friday's father were healthy and well again, Crusoe shared with them his idea of escaping from the island. Friday's father too confirmed that Crusoe would be treated with a lot of love and affection on his island. The Spaniard too wanted to get back to his people, who were apparently without food and at the mercy of the savages for a long time. Moreover, the Spaniards who were still living on the mainland did not have the necessary tools which could help them to escape.

Crusoe offered his own services at once, and promised to find a way in which they could all escape. The Spaniard declared that he and his men would forever be grateful to Crusoe, if the sailor could help them get back to their own country. Robinson Crusoe therefore, offered to build a boat by which the Spaniard and Friday's father could get back to the mainland and rejoin their people.

The Spaniard however, suggested that he wait with Crusoe for another few months, so that he could take back some food for the natives and his own people still living on the island. He offered his own, and Friday's father's help in plowing more crops, so that there was enough food for everyone once they all came back.

Soon, all four men got ready in making all the necessary preparations. Bread was baked in great numbers, the meat too was made ready and grapes were dried into raisins. After six whole months, it was time for the Spaniard and Friday's father to go back and bring back their people to Robinson Crusoe's island.

The Spaniard knew how to sail on Crusoe's canoe and Friday's father too learnt everything rather quickly. With an eight-day provision

of food and water, the men set off for the mainland. Crusoe had even given them a supply of muskets and gunpowder, which were to be used only in the event of some emergency. And Crusoe even instructed the Spaniard to fire his musket twice when they would come back, signaling to Crusoe the arrival of friends and not enemies.

Twenty-eight years had now passed since Robinson Crusoe first arrived on the island. However, things now looked to change. If everything went according to plan, Robinson Crusoe would soon be headed back home, to England.

Chapter Twelve

Englishmen

It was eight days later, when Robinson Crusoe was pulled out of bed by an extremely excited Friday. "Master, canoe arrive, friends arrive."

Crusoe, now extremely hopeful about his possible return to England, came rushing out of the fortress and ran up the hill. However, even as he saw the boat coming towards the island, he realised that the ship was not coming from the mainland, but from the sea.

"You fool! These are not our friends. Quick, hide here, and let me find out who these people are!" Even as they tried to hide, Robinson Crusoe took out his spy glass and took a good look at the people coming towards the island. But even before he could do that, he caught the glimpse of ship anchored a little away from the beach. From the looks of it, it seemed that the ship was a merchant vessel from England and the people in the boat were coming from the same ship.

Robinson Crusoe's emotions were mixed with joy and worry. He definitely was happy to see his own people, Englishmen, coming towards the island. But at the same time he knew that there was no reason for the ship to be in this region. There had been no storms either, for the ship to have lost its course. He therefore decided to keep a watch on the men and find out what their intentions were.

The tide was moving towards the island and so the boat soon came up along the beach. However, things did not look too bright. For of the fourteen people on board the boat, three of them seemed to be travelling as prisoners.

As soon as the boat was on the beach, the prisoners were pulled out of the boat and were cut loose. One of the prisoners, clearly an Englishman, fell at the feet of the sailors there and started to plead. He was merely kicked away, as he fell back on the sand.

Friday too had been watching the entire spectacle unfold before him and he asked Crusoe, "Englishman also murder and eat man?"

Crusoe was quite disgusted with this question and he barked back, "They might be murdered, yes... but rest assured, these prisoners aren't going to be eaten."

Crusoe continued to watch the events on the beach. He desperately wanted to save the Englishmen, but he knew that he would have to plan his next move very carefully.

Fortunately, six of the sailors who had arrived there, went off deep into the island, leaving the prisoners guarded by only two drunk sailors. The prisoners however, had nowhere to run and therefore, they remained under the tree, apparently waiting for their end.

"Enough!" exclaimed Robinson Crusoe. "Let's get to it now, man!" he declared, as both he and Friday started to load their muskets, shotgun and pistols. They then got off the hill and made off towards the beach.

As their guards were now fast asleep in the long boat, Crusoe and Friday quietly went to where the prisoners were sitting. Not wanting to wake up the sleeping sailors in the boat, Crusoe softly whispered, "What seems to be the matter, gentlemen?"

The prisoners turned around at once, completely shocked to their very bones to hear someone speak to them in perfect English. But the moment their eyes fell on Crusoe, they were first quite shocked to see a bearded white man standing before them, in clothes made from goatskin. Their hopes of meeting their saviour immediately seemed to wash away.

Crusoe could understand this from the way in which their expressions changed, and he assured them, "Do not be alarmed. I am a fellow Englishman and I am here to help you."

This cheered the prisoners a little bit and then, one of the prisoners, an aged man came before Robinson Crusoe and said, "You must have spotted the ship anchored a little away from here… well, I am… rather was, the captain of that ship. And instead of murdering me after their little mutiny, my own sailors decided to leave me, my first mate and this passenger, here on the island. Oh, our deaths shall surely be slow and painful, living all alone on this deserted island."

Robinson Crusoe started laughing on hearing of their tales of despair, and he replied, "I should be a ghost by that logic… I was stranded on this island some twenty-eight years ago, and here I am, coming to your rescue. Now quickly, we must get out of here before the remaining sailors come back. Come quietly, and do as I tell you to."

Crusoe and Friday quickly led the English seamen through the woods, till they were hidden safely by the jungle cover. Then turning to the Captain of the ship, Crusoe asked, "I can help you get your ship back. I have enough arms and ammunition for that. But after that, will you do something for me?"

"Anything, my good man, and everything," replied the Captain. "I will place myself and the services of my entire ship at your disposal." His first mate and the gentleman who had been on board simply as a passenger too nodded their heads, agreeing to what their captain was saying.

"Alright then, I shall help you. But remember, I know this island way better than you do, and therefore, you must do exactly as I tell you to," declared Robinson Crusoe right at the beginning of their negotiations. "And once we are successful, do you swear to take me and my man here, Friday, back to London with you?

Remember, we do not have any money to pay for our passage back home."

The Captain almost looked embarrassed on hearing Crusoe's words and he quickly yelled, "You must be out of your mind, kind Sir! You will have done me a huge favour. This is the least that I can do for you!"

Crusoe nodded his head, acknowledging the Captain's assurance. "Fair enough! Now, if we are to get your ship back, we need to move fast!"

The Captain was a kind man, and he asked Crusoe to spare the life of the sailors who had come with them to the island in the boat. "However, we also have to make sure that they don't exactly run back and warn their mates back on board the ship."

"There is only one way to buy their silence," said Crusoe gently, and he handed each of the people gathered there a gun. It was clear enough — the sailors would just have to be shot.

All it took was the death of two revolting sailors to cause the other's to give up their mutiny

and swear allegiance to the Captain. The Captain agreed to spare the lives — but only on the condition that they all work with him to reclaim his ship.

The prisoner sailors were then dragged back to Crusoe's fortress, where they were kept concealed inside the cave. Crusoe and the Captain then discussed what they should do next, so as to take back control of the ship.

"We are just five people and there are still around twenty-six people on board the ship. How on earth are we ever going to win against those odds?" lamented the Captain.

Crusoe too nodded in agreement. "These men all know that if they are defeated, they will meet the laws of mutiny and will be hanged to their death. And therefore, these people will be desperate to win against us. No, we must think of another way… we must think of some way in which we can trap them."

Chapter Thirteen

Turning the Tables

Though they were discussing their next strategy for quite some time now, yet Robinson Crusoe and his new found friends weren't exactly able to come up with something that would surely turn the tide in their favour.

Suddenly, the Captain sprang up and said, "What fools we have been to have not spotted the obvious! The sailors on board the ship will surely come to the island in a short while. After all, we still have their friends. Maybe we can spring our trap on them at that time."

And the Captain was indeed right. Because even as they hit upon this idea, the ship started

to fire her cannons and hoisted several flags, each time signaling to their men on the island to come back on board. However, no boat stirred at the beach.

Crusoe ran up to the hill and with his spyglass, he kept constant vigil on the activities on the ship. As was expected, Crusoe spotted another boat being put down into the water and ten seamen, all armed with guns and muskets, heading towards the shore. The Captain took a look at the boat through the spyglass as well, and he identified the men who were now on their way to land.

"You see those three men sitting towards the stern? They are true, honest seamen and they must have been forced to become a part of this horrible mutiny. I am sure they will not offer us much resistance. But the other seven, including their officer... well, they're villains, each and every one of them."

"Then the numbers are in our favour," declared Crusoe, grinning in joy. "We are five people, there are two prisoners sitting in the cave as we speak who you say can be trusted. So it'll be seven against ten... or rather, ten against seven, considering the three men in the boat are honest sailors."

The two loyal prisoners were immediately set free and once everyone was properly armed, the contingent led by Crusoe started to make their way down to the beach.

The sailors from the ship had already reached the shore and were walking around along the beach. They fired several rounds in the air, prompting their shipmates to come back to them. But it was of no use. Finally, seven of them decided to form a search party and go into the interior of the island, whereas three of the men were left to guard the boat.

On noting their actions, Crusoe turned to his friends and said, "We have to make a choice. If we capture the seven people searching the island, then these three will run back to the ship and that

will be the end of it all. Rather, I suggest that we first nab the three by the boat and take the boat in our custody too."

As per their strategy, Friday and two of their men ran up to the crest of a hill and started yelling "Hello". This led the sailors to think that their shipmates were calling out to them. Catching their attention, Friday and the two loyal sailors started running deeper into the island, across the creek.

The men decided to sail around the creek in their boat, but since the high tide was now coming into the island, the boat proved to be completely useless. Therefore, the boat was dragged along to the creek, after which the sailors got into it and rowed over to the other side. As they got out, two people were left to guard the boat and the remaining eight went out in search of their friends.

Everything moved exactly as Robinson Crusoe had planned it. As soon the search party moved out of sight, Crusoe and his friends ran

towards the boat and aimed their guns at the surprised sailors. They saw that they were greatly outnumbered and therefore, they surrendered at once. The Captain immediately came forward and vouched for the two honest soldiers' loyalty, who too were happy to see the Captain again and agreed to join his sides to fight against those sailors who had taken part in the mutiny.

They were soon joined by Friday and the two sailors, who claimed that the search party had been led deep into the jungle, where they were now completely lost. It would take till nightfall for them to come back to the creek. This just made it easier for Crusoe to form the rest of his plans.

When the sailors did reach the creek, they were tired to their very bones and were in an extremely foul mood. And their mood turned to that of shock and surprise, when they noticed two more of their shipmates missing. They started running in ever direction frantically, calling out to their men.

As they started to split up, Crusoe and his men took their position. The commander of the sailors, the man who had instigated the mutiny, came upon a large rock. He did not notice the Captain standing above it and as soon as he was in range, the Captain fired his pistol, killing the villain at once.

With their leader dead, Crusoe and his men branched out at once and in a circular manner, they surrounded the rest of the seven sailors. Crusoe decided to first offer the men the terms of surrender, before striking them dead.

"Tom Smith? This is me, Williams!" cried on the loyalist sailors.

A voice called out from behind some bushes, "Where in the blazes are ye Williams? We're searching everywhere for ye!"

Williams continued, "I am offering you terms of surrender. Drop your weapons and raise your hands."

"Surrender?" cried Smith, completely taken aback. "Who are we surrendering to, and why on earth are we surrendering?"

"To our Captain," called out Williams, "and his fifty friends. They took me prisoner too. Come on now, save yourselves mate! The leader of the mutiny is already dead. You can check if you don't believe me!"

Smith started shivering out of fright on hearing about how vastly they were outnumbered. "And our lives? Will we be killed once we surrender?"

"No, your lives will be spared. Only Will Atkins is doomed and he won't meet the same fate as you'll. Come on now, hurry up!" ordered the loyal Williams.

On hearing these words, Will Atkins screamed, "What on earth are you talking about? Why am I being treated any differently than the rest of these people?"

"Because you attacked me the moment the mutiny began," responded the Captain this time.

"For you, I have a very special end planned. Unless of course, the Governor of this island convinces me otherwise."

Crusoe relished this moment. As he mulled over the Captain's last words, he thought to himself, "Come to think of it, I am the governor of the island. It just never struck me." However, the sailors had started to throw their weapons away and therefore, Crusoe immediately sent out Friday and the two loyalist sailors to tie up their prisoners.

The men were quickly bound and carried back to the cave, where the joined the rest of the prisoners. Crusoe pretended telling his 'fifty' soldiers to stay hidden, as he did not want that lie to be exposed. He also made sure that he did not come before the prisoners, lest they formed a low opinion about the Governor dressed in goat skin clothes.

Once the prisoners were all in the cave, they all begged for mercy, asking the Captain to spare

their lives. But the Captain merely replied, "We'll have to wait and see what the Governor decides for you. Your lives are not in my hands."

Will Atkins quickly fell at the Captain's feet and pleaded, "Oh please kind Sir, please ask the Governor to spare my life. I didn't mean any harm, Sir, it was just that I was taken over by the mutiny. Please Sir, I am begging you…"

The Captain was naturally relishing all this.

As the Captain went out, he stumbled over someone and fell to the ground. As he looked up, he saw the Governor, kneeled down before him, milking his goats!

Chapter Fourteen

Taking Back the Ship

The Captain and Robinson Crusoe went out at once, so as to discuss their new plans — now they needed to take the ship back in their power. Both the Captain and Crusoe were of the same opinion that taking out some ten men, and taking out the mutineers on the ship were not the same thing. There force of seven soldiers would never win this battle.

There was only one thing left to do. The Captain went back into the cave and turning to his prisoners, he said, "Either you all will die on this island, or go back to England and face trial

for mutiny. But yes, there is one way out for all of you."

The prisoners immediately looked up at the Captain, their hopes lit once again. "What is it? Please tell us... we will do anything to survive."

"Well, you will have to then come with me and fight with me to take back control of my ship. Only under these conditions has the Governor agreed to spare your lives."

Naturally the men agreed to this proposal at once. Who wouldn't want to save their lives, after all! Hearing them pledge their loyalty to him, the Captain rushed back to Crusoe and told him of this new development.

"Fair enough!" exclaimed Crusoe. "However, we must make sure that they are true to their word. We'll keep five of the prisoners here, in the cave, while the rest can go to fight with you. That way, if they return to their revolting ways, we will kill the five prisoners here."

The Captain was extremely appreciative of this idea, and he went back to tell the prisoners of the same. The prisoners immediately started begging and pleading their friends not to turn their backs on the Captain, else they would meet with their end in the cave.

As night fell, Crusoe and Friday helped the Captain and his men get up on the boat and sail off towards the ship. They themselves remained on the island with the rest of the prisoners. The sailors aboard the ship were of the opinion that their comrades were coming back, and therefore, they were completely off guard when the Captain and his men began their attack.

The Captain charged after the man who had started the mutiny and after some heavy firing, the sailor lay there on the deck, dead. The rest of the sailors who were still a part of the mutiny immediately surrendered. The ship was now once again back in the Captain's control.

As soon as the Captain took control of his ship, he fired seven canons into the sea, signaling to an overjoyed Crusoe that the battle had been won.

At day break, the victorious Captain returned to the shore and embraced Crusoe, saying, "You have kept your word, o noble gentleman... and now I keep mine. The ship is yours, the ship's Captain is yours and so are all the sailors on board!"

Robinson Crusoe did not say anything. He just continued to look at the ship. This was the vessel that was finally going to take him back home, after a long wait of twenty-eight years. However much tried, Crusoe could not hold back his tears, as he hugged the Captain, his saviour.

There were joyous celebrations on the island that day. The Captain had brought back a huge supply of wine, meat, biscuits and vegetables. He made a personal gift of a set of beautiful clothes to Crusoe, who had almost given up any hope of wearing proper linen clothes again. Though truth be told, he did feel very uncomfortable in his new clothes. After all, the goat skin had almost become his second skin in the all the years that he had spent on the island.

Then the question arose of the prisoners from the mutiny. All the sailors had shifted their allegiance to the Captain, barring two of them, who still believed that the Captain should be deposed. "What are we to do with them?" the Captain asked for Crusoe's advice. "We could take them back, bound and gagged in the hold on the ship, but you never know what trouble they might later cause."

Crusoe thought about the Captain's words for a while and then he was struck with a wonderful idea. "I think we should leave them on the island. After all, if I could survive, then I am sure they can too."

The Captain liked the idea very much and he sent for the prisoner's at once. They were finally

going to meet the Governor, particularly since he was now properly dressed to play the part of one.

The moment the two prisoners came before Crusoe, the "Governor" began, "I have been told of all that you have done aboard my friend, the Captain's ship. And now that you have been arrested for your villainous acts, I think you too should meet the same fate as your leaders. Should I hang you? Should I have you both killed as pirates? Go on, tell me… you know I can do anything I like with you since I am after all the Governor of this island."

One of the prisoners immediately fell to his feet and begged, "Mercy, your Excellency, we beg for mercy!"

Crusoe seemed to ponder over their fate and he replied, "Well, you see, I am going back to England in the ship, with the Captain and the rest of the crew. You can come with us, clapped in irons of course, and then, once we land on British soil, you'll will be tried for mutiny. And

that is awarded with the death penalty. So either way you will all die. Unless of course, you all stay back on this island. I don't think there is any other way out for you."

The men were extremely pleased with the offer that Crusoe made them. They quickly replied, "Of course, we shall stay back on this island. We would like that very much."

Crusoe now only wanted to go back home. He did not much care about the mutiny, or about fighting any more battles, or killing any more men. The men were agreeable to stay on the island, so he couldn't care about them anymore.

The next few hours was spent in Crusoe telling them everything they needed to know to survive on the island. He told them about his own experiences, right from the time he built his own fort, to the time he baked his own bread, to when he built his own canoe. The men eagerly listened to him, for this knowledge would help them save their lives on the island.

Robinson Crusoe also made mention of his friends, the Spaniards and Friday's father, who were expected on the island in a few days. The men promised to welcome them warmly and to treat them with respect.

That night, Robinson Crusoe did not sleep even a wink. He instead chose to roam around the island. Now that he was finally ready to leave the island and go back home, he felt a little sad.

The next morning, the long boat from the ship came to the shore to take Robinson Crusoe and Friday to the ship. Crusoe carried with him his goatskin cap, the umbrella that he had made from goat skin, and also his parrots, along with all the gold and silver sacks that he had found from a sinking ship a few years back.

As he made the last entry on his log calendar, Robinson Crusoe recorded he was going back to England on the 19th of December, 1686, after twenty-eight years, two months and nine days on the island.

Chapter Fifteen

England!

It was another six months, till the 11th of June, 1687, that Robinson Crusoe arrived in London, with Friday. In all, he was returning home after a total of thirty-five years away from home.

The first thing that he did was go back home, to Yorkshire to be united with his family. However, as he had expected, his parents were both dead. He did manage to establish links with his two sisters and also the sons of his brother, who too had passed away a few years back.

Crusoe immediately put his mind to work, making several trip to Portugal in the years since.

He revived his plantation business in Brazil in this process. The men who he had entrusted his business to had increased the success of the plantation manifold in his absence. A large sum of money was therefore accrued for him, which was then transferred to his bankers in England.

Crusoe did have the niggling intention of perhaps going back to Brazil and taking up his plantation business again. But he decided against it, and instead sold his entire property there to two of his neighbouring farmers, thereby deciding to stay in England.

Robinson Crusoe took under his wing his brother's two sons. One was studying law, while it seemed the other one longed to travel, quite like his uncle, the great adventurer, Robinson Crusoe. Crusoe made sure that his wishes were met with and in five years time, his nephew became one of the most well-known merchants of the seas.

Therefore, it was after eight whole years that Robinson Crusoe and Friday, went aboard his nephew's ship, for a trip to South America.

Since it was not far from their original course, Crusoe decided to visit his old island once. When he reached there, he was in for quite a surprise. His little uninhabited island had now become a full-fledged colony. The Englishmen had worked along with the Spaniards and together, they had started a civilization on the island.

He learnt that the Spaniards had managed to bring back most of their men and women from the mainland in these eight years that Crusoe was in England and now there were more than twenty children running about, playing on the island.

On the insistence of the Spaniards and the Englishmen, Robinson Crusoe, the first "Governor" of the island, stayed there for a whole month. He supplied the people on the island with many goods and commodities that he was carrying with him on board his ship. More importantly, he even left behind a blacksmith and a carpenter on the island, thereby helping the people there to expand their colony manifold.

In the next few years, Robinson Crusoe and Friday made many more trips to the island, bringing back more and more supplies with them each and every time. He also brought in many more people, all of whom had expressed a desire to live on the island, thereby helping the island grow manifold over the years.

And with each new voyage, each new adventure that he undertook between England, Brazil and his island, Robinson Crusoe always had fond memories of his first great adventure, one that lasted for twenty-eight years, making him live as the Governor of his own little island.

About the Author

■ Daniel Defoe

Daniel Defoe, the great English novelist, was born Daniel Foe sometime between 1659 and 1661. His parents were Alice and James Foe and it is believed he was born in St. Giles Cripplegate London. As a Presbyterian Dissenter, not conforming to the services of the Church of England, Defoe chose to become a merchant and traded in hosiery, woolens and other such ware. He was to become a writer, journalist and a pamphleteer.

As a pamphleteer and political activist, Daniel Defoe was imprisoned for his sensational essays. He is believed to be one of the earliest proponents of the English novel and was responsible for popularising it among the reading masses. He is known as the founder of the English novel, and *The Adventures of Robinson Crusoe*, is his most distinguishing work.

■ Characters

Robinson Crusoe: He is the narrator of the tale. At the beginning of the novel, he is a young man in search of a career. Rejecting his father's suggestion of a career in Law, Crusoe decides to become a merchant at sea. All through his stay at the deserted island, he shows great strength of character and presence of mind. His remarkable perseverance takes him through a twenty-eight-year isolation on the island.

Friday: Friday is a young man, a native of the Caribbean. He is a savage, a cannibal, who is saved by Crusoe when he is about to be eaten by other savages. He turns to more civilized ways after staying with Crusoe. Friday is fiercely loyal to Crusoe and would lay down his life for his master without a thought.

■ Questions

Chapter 1
- What profession did Robinson Crusoe's father want him to pursue?
- How did Robinson's dream of sailing come true?
- Describe his time at the sugar plantations.

Chapter 2
- What commodities did Robinson take on the ship for trade?
- What was the fate of the ship at sea?
- Describe Crusoe's experience with the fierce sea storm.

Chapter 3
- How did Crusoe manage to salvage some supplies from the wrecked ship?
- Who were his only four companions on the island?
- How did Crusoe mark time?

Chapter 4
- Where and how did Crusoe build his hut?
- How did he plan his food on the island?
- What did he do for storage of grains?
- How did he bake bread?

Chapter 5
- Why did Robinson Crusoe plan to build a canoe? What happened to the canoe?
- How did he fashion new clothes for himself?
- Was the second canoe a success? How?

Chapter 6
- What ingenuous methods did Crusoe devise to catch prey?

THE ADVENTURES OF ROBINSON CRUSOE

- How did he increase the livestock at his farm?
- What was it that indicated another human life on the island?

Chapter 7

- Describe the sight that greeted Crusoe at the bottom of the hill.
- What was his reaction to seeing the signs of cannibalism?

Chapter 8

- What did Robinson Crusoe find aboard the Spanish ship?
- What dream did Crusoe see?
- Describe how Crusoe and the native came together.

Chapter 9

- Why did Crusoe name the native 'Friday'?
- What kind of relationship developed between the two?
- How did Crusoe help Friday become more civilized?

Chapter 10

- Describe Crusoe's and Friday's second run-in with the cannibals.
- Were they able to save the Spaniard?

Chapter 11

- Who was the second person they saved?
- What plans did Crusoe make with the Spaniard?

Chapter 12

- Who were the Englishmen who arrived at Crusoe's island?
- What had taken place on the ship? Who were the prisoners?

Chapter 13

- How did Crusoe help the Captain capture the mates on the island?

THE ADVENTURES OF ROBINSON CRUSOE

Chapter 14
- *How did Crusoe manage to win back the Captain's ship for him?*
- *What deal was offered to the prisoners by Crusoe?*

Chapter 15
- *What did Robinson find in London?*
- *What did he do with his plantation business?*
- *What happened to Crusoe's island?*